DAMIEN

CUNNINGHAM

A portion of proceeds from this book will be donated to the Friends of the Fisher House. The Fisher Houses are dedicated to providing comfort and relief to families of hospitalized veterans.

J James C Boland Author

Richard Flatley Illustrator

Dedicated To

Brian P. Boland

Table of Contents

October, 2020

Chapter 1

It was late fall of 2012 when I went for a walk at Forest Home Cemetery in Forest Park, IL.

I belonged to a group called The Windy City Explorers, and a walk through the cemetery was scheduled for the day. The Windy City Explorers is a Meet-Up group founded by a lawyer named Tom Besore. He picks out various sites of interest in and around the city of Chicago that he posts online and invites members of the group to join for a walk. He researches the sites, and his narratives are always informative.

The walks are very popular and often draw as many as 150 people signing up. One notable walk was called the "Seven Bridges Walk." On that walk, we went from one bridge after another along the Chicago River. The bridges would open, one after the other, to allow boats to travel down on their way to portage in Lake Michigan. I remember one time the Seven Bridges Walk was scheduled for the same day as Chicago's St. Patrick's Day celebration. There we were, around 150 members of the Meet-Up trying to assemble in a crowd of thousands of celebrants. We somehow managed to walk to each of the opened bridges, along with a thousand other people who joined us. I think they were just following along with us thinking it was part of the St. Patrick's celebration.

I have walked through many Chicago and nearby suburban neighborhoods, churches and cemeteries. Two of the cemeteries, like Rosehill and Graceland, are among the city's oldest and most historic. Many of the city's streets are named after Chicagoans who are buried in those two cemeteries. Graceland Cemetery, for example, holds the remains of Marshall Field and George Pullman along with sports figures, political leaders, authors, architects, celebrities and others. Graceland Cemetery, on the north-side of Chicago, was opened around 1860, and as you may imagine, one can easily get lost wandering around the thousands of historic graves. Regrettably, outside the upkeep by the caretakers of old cemeteries, most graves are neglected and forgotten.

Chapter 2

I was especially interested in the Meet-Up walk in the Forest Home Cemetery. You see, the Historic Societies of the towns of Oak Park and Forest Park had collaborated to use reenactors to stand near the graves of a few deceased people and give a firsthand account of their lives. The idea was to bring to life, through the reenactments, what the deceased may say if they could talk. It was as though the deceased were standing there in front of us, in period dress, relating events of their past lives. It was a wonderful idea and one that I really looked forward to attending. The event was scheduled for a late fall Sunday in October of 2012. At the time, I was a full-time teacher on Chicago's near north-side and had passed by the Forest Home Cemetery without ever having pulled into it.

On Sunday around 11:30 in the morning, I drove over to the Forest Home Cemetery, anxious to observe the reenactments. Arriving at noon, I quickly realized I could not park on the street adjacent from the entrance. It was a busy street, and cars had parked on both sides. At first, I was concerned that the cemetery would be crowded but then realized it was probably from the many apartment buildings across from the cemetery.

Slowing down as I began to pass the entrance, I saw that there was an iron gate and a narrow concrete drive leading into the cemetery. Historically, the cemetery was built on the site of a Potawatomi Indian burial ground until 1835. Then, in 1876, the Forest Home Cemetery was formally established there.

Pulling in through the old iron gate, I drove down a single-lane, old concrete drive. Parking my car down the narrow concrete road, I had to pull up on the grass bordering the road since it was only wide enough for one car. Stepping out onto the road, I could see it was in terrible shape. The concrete road was broken with grass growing up in the middle. Getting out of my car, I stood there a moment and tried to imagine the many horse-drawn hearses that had pulled into the cemetery and gone down this very same road. When in a cemetery, I always think of the sadness felt by others as they came to see their loved ones off to eternity. I often look at graves and think of the mourning and tears shed by grievers.

I pulled my collar up as it seemed a bit on the cool side, and the sky was dark gray. Leaves were blowing across the road, and I looked around to see if I could see anybody. At that, I soon recognized a few people from my Meet-Up group as they were walking south and following some arrows that had been set up in the ground. Catching up to them, we all agreed that listening to reenactors was a great idea, and we all hoped to learn something today.

Up ahead to our right, we soon saw our first reenactor standing by herself along a grave around 200 feet to our right.

Approaching her, we could see by her grave that it was Emma Goldman. She nodded to us as we smiled back, and I could see she was dressed in black, including a black hat and a black face veil. Her dress was down just past her knees, and I could see even her shoes and gloves were black.

As she began to speak, I soon learned that Ms. Goldman had been born in Lithuania. She emigrated to the US at a young age and acknowledged being an anarchist. Taking us through life around the turn of the 20th century, we learned of her study of Marxism and embracing left-wing ideals. We learned that through her writings and speeches, she was a leading advocate of social reform. After a few minutes, she began to conclude as more visitors began to gather around waiting for her to begin a new presentation. I couldn't help but be impressed by these reenactors, for they had obviously researched their subjects.

Chapter 3

Continuing along, I noticed an arrow pointing off to the far right, where another reenactment was taking place. As I approached, I could see the reenactor had a straw hat, long-sleeved striped shirt, dark trousers and a blood-stained butcher apron. He had a big dark mustache, bushy eyebrows, and in his hand was a big knife with a dark red stain. We gathered around him, and he recounted to us his name and informed us that he had been accused of having killed his wife. As I recall, it happened in the 1880s on the north-side of Chicago. He and his wife were emigrants and had opened a butcher shop. After four years in business, she disappeared and was never seen again. His account was that she had gone up to Milwaukee to visit her sister and not returned. Several of his customers, alarmed at her absence, had notified the police of their concern.

The police had stopped by his shop to discuss his wife's disappearance, which caused him a great deal of distress. He informed us that he was working on a big catering order when the police came in to question him. The police quizzed him, looked around, and were ready to walk outside. It was then, however, that one of them asked if he had a basement.

Responding in the affirmative, the police then asked how to access the basement.

Reluctantly, he pointed to a door under a set of stairs leading up to the second floor. Opening the door, two of the officers, lighting a kerosene lantern, began to slowly descend into the basement. The butcher remained upstairs under the watchful eye of a third officer of the law.

Looking around the basement, the first thing they observed was a big wooden table, next to a huge meat grinder. At first, nothing seemed out of order. The place had a smell of blood which, of course, was to be expected in a butcher shop. Then they noticed a female's dress hanging off a hook against the wall. That seemed odd but no cause for concern as it was assumed that the wife had probably been down here working at some point in the near past.

Then one of the police officers noticed something on the floor under the table. Reaching down to pick it up, he dropped it back onto the floor. Shining the lantern down on it, they quickly realized it was a human hand with a ring on one of its fingers. They instantly knew who it belonged to… the missing wife. It had to be her hand. Neighbors identified the ring as belonging to the butcher's wife.

The butcher was taken into custody and was soon indicted in his wife's apparent murder. At his trial, his only defense was his plea, "I didn't do it. I didn't do it." Court reporters wrote that he was found guilty, sentenced to death by hanging, and as he was led out of court, they could hear him over and over repeat the same words, "I didn't do it."

The butcher was in prison awaiting his execution when he had a fatal heart attack and died. The coroner ruled that his heart attack was probably due to the fact that the butcher had been known to chew on uncooked bacon fat most of his life. Too much cholesterol was listed as cause of death.

So now, as I stood there with a half dozen other spectators, the reenactor did an admirable job reciting facts to us as the butcher.

Standing there, holding the bloody knife in front of us, he kept repeating, "I didn't do it. I didn't do it."

After the butcher's death in 1888, he was interned in Forest Home Cemetery. To those of us who heard his words denying his involvement in his wife's death, you have to wonder, if he didn't do it, then who did? How did his wife's hand end up on the floor beneath the table in the basement?

Chapter 4

The afternoon was passing too quickly, and it was almost 3:45. The cemetery gate would automatically close and lock at 4:30.

I wanted to see at least one more reenactor, as their performances were outstanding. Off in the distance, I could see a few spectators gathered around another grave. Walking over there with a few others, we had to wait for a chance to draw close. After a few minutes, the reenactors concluded a presentation, and we approached three young woman around the age of 17-19. Looking at them, I could see they were dressed in long dresses that reached down to their ankles. They did not have hats, but their long hair looked wet and reached down past their shoulders. The three of them had a look of sadness upon their young faces, which led me to believe they were great actors.

They introduced themselves as victims of the SS Eastland disaster of 1915. They had been employed by the Western Electric company in Cicero, IL and had signed up for a company picnic to be held on July 15, 1915. Over 2500 people had gathered early that day for the much-anticipated picnic, and there was a genuine air of excitement. Many of the 2500 were families and friends, and they were all looking forward that day to the SS Eastland heading out on Lake Michigan. Their destination was Michigan City, Indiana, and for many of those gathering on the ship, it was their first time in downtown Chicago. The ship was tied up along the Clark Street Bridge, and as more and more carriages and trolleys showed up, the area became congested.

Across the river was a big red-brick building with a clock tower at the top. That building was to play a pivotal role that day as a morgue. Today, that building is still there, on the north bank of the Chicago River.

As the three young ladies began to recount to us, the ship had been improperly ballasted when most of the 2500 people aboard stood on the port side to wave at family and friends. Suddenly, the ship turned over. It happened so suddenly that hundreds of people were caught below decks while others on the main deck were caught in the undertow of the ship flipping over. Family members along the shore were stunned to see what happened and did not know what to do. The screams could be heard throughout the downtown area. Life preservers were thrown into the water but had little positive effect. Rescuers began to arrive, but they, too, did not know what to do as this had never happened before.

As bodies were recovered, they were brought over to the multi-story red-brick building across the river. At a nearby armory, hundreds of bodies were laid out on the concrete floor to be identified. It was unimaginable chaos, confusion and terror. The end result was that over 800 people drowned, and it all happened on a lovely Saturday summer morning. The grief felt and expressed by fellow workers, family and neighbors was beyond comfort. I wanted to believe that this couldn't have happened.

Entire families were lost that horrible July 1915 morning.

Of the 800 victims, 65 were buried at the Forest Home Cemetery.

The three re-enactors I saw that fall day in 2012 now represented the short lives of Eastland disaster victims.

Standing there listening to them recount the horror of that terrible morning 97 years earlier was so sad. The three young ladies looked so forlorn, so wet-looking, so full of recognition that their lives were cut short. They had never grown up to marry, have children, or grandchildren and live out all that life had offered them prior to that tragic July 15.

The three young girls eloquently expressed how they had been forgotten out here in the cemetery. Their families had been lost that tragic day, and the few who survived had visited them early on, but over the years, they too had passed. Now, for too many years, they have laid alone, forgotten and full of remorse over having never lived to adulthood. As they concluded their presentation, there was complete silence as those of us witnessing their recounting that morning felt shared grief. I know, for myself, I walked away with my head bent, my throat choked and tears filling my eyes.

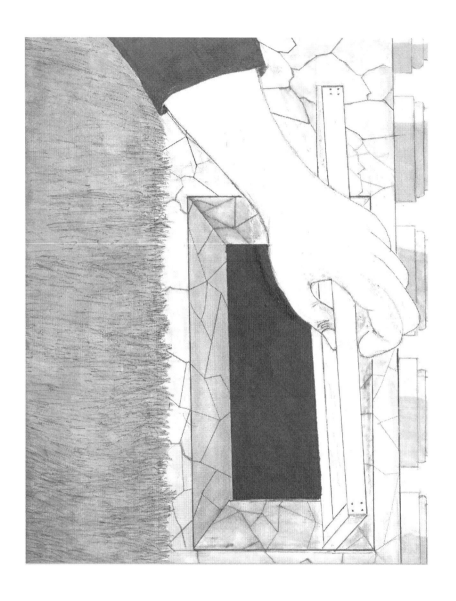

Chapter 5

Slowly walking away from the Eastland disaster reenactors, I had lost track of time. It was only upon hearing Tom Besore calling out to us that we must head to the entrance that I came back to reality. Quietly walking across the brown grass, still thinking of those poor victims of the Eastland disaster, I could see the reenactors had packed up and they too, were heading toward the old iron gate.

There was something that had triggered a reaction in me to want to learn more. When I had arrived, I had seen a huge monument with the name Cunningham engraved in stone at the top and heard that nobody had been buried there. So, while everybody headed toward the exit, I decided to take a quick walk over to the Cunningham mausoleum. Approaching it, I felt a bit of nervousness in knowing that the gate would close soon and I could get stuck overnight in the Forest Home Cemetery.

As it was late fall, the sky was darkening, and the wind was picking up as I stood in front of the monument and climbed the first few steps onto the stone platform. Walking behind the upright stone tablet, which was intended to show who was buried there, I could see a broad, flat concrete pad which stood about a foot and a half above ground. Leaves were blowing across it, and there were a few dead branches strewn about.

Stepping down, I noticed that there were a few windows just above the ground, looking into the crypt beneath. In fact, there were two windows each with three panes of glass with iron bars in front.

Walking along to the rear of the platform, I saw there were steps leading down to a rusty iron door and a big rusty key lock. The stairs did not look inviting, as they appeared damp, dark and covered with leafs. I knew that the steps and the iron door must lead into the crypt. I thought to myself that it could be that nobody had entered this crypt in 100 years. After all, since it was empty and the Cunninghams had moved away, why would it have ever been opened?

Ever aware of the limited time, I walked back to the side windows. They were dirty and covered by dried leaves that the wind had blown up against them. The windows were recessed, and I noticed one of them had no bars. Taking the toe of my shoe, I pushed against the window and was surprised to see it open. I couldn't believe my eyes that the window would open inward. Bending down, I couldn't see inside, so I lowered myself to one knee to peek inside, but it was too low to the ground to look inside.

Now, being extremely curious, I laid prone on the leaf-covered ground. I took my cell phone, turned on the flashlight, and with one hand pushing the dirty window inward, I tried to look inside. The first thing I noticed was the strong scent coming out from the crypt. It was a cool, damp smell with a hint of sulfur. I tried holding my breath out of fear that maybe breathing in the air might be harmful. I had once seen a movie where an ancient Egyptian tomb had been opened, and the air caused those breathing it to come down with a fatal disease. So, I peered in while holding my breath.

Just as my eyes became used to the dark, I moved my flashlight around to see what was down there. Then I saw it, a coffin sitting on a wheel-less bier. The coffin lid, I could see, was raised and twisted sideways.

I was so entranced at what I was looking at that I didn't pick up on the sound of crunched leaves right behind me. To this day, I don't know whether I heard the sound of the leaves or the sound of a voice first, but this I know, I heard a crackly voice say, "There is nobody down there."

Quickly turning around to see where this voice was coming from, I saw him. He was a young man in a frayed dark topcoat, a faded yellowish white shirt, dark pants and dark shoes. He was kind of stooped and appeared very old, but I could discern he was young. I think I knew he was young by the boyish look on his wrinkled face and the light in his dark eyes. His face was a deep dark red, his black hair seemed to spike upwards, and his voice was not just raspy but creaky-like.

As he reached his bony hand out, I almost pulled away from touching him. In touching his hand, I felt as though I was touching the crispy skin of a Thanksgiving turkey. After holding my breath while looking into the crypt, I now could breathe deeply, and in doing so, I picked up a strong burnt smell. Who was this man? What was he doing out here in the cemetery? Was he alone? I felt an uncertainty, knowing I was alone with him with the cemetery ready to close. How do I get away from him? I kept thinking, now is not the time for a conversation, and it seemed obvious he wanted me to talk.

I began to edge away from him, but he kept plying me with questions. He asked, "Do you come out here often? What is your name? Where do you live? How did you get here? Why do you have to leave? Can you stay a little longer? Are you coming back?"

To his last question, I informed him that I had to leave since my car was parked inside the cemetery and it was almost 4:30. As I said that, I turned my back to him and began to run away down the cement roadway towards my car.

Getting inside, I fumbled for my key, put the car in Drive and realized I had to turn it around to get back to the entrance/exit. I didn't want to run over a grave in the grassy area, and so I had to back and forth my car until I could make a turn. At that, I sped down the narrow, old concrete road, and I could see the huge iron gates just as they slowly began to close. Without slowing down, I sped right through the narrow opening out on to a busy street. A car honked at me as I did a right turn, but all I cared about was getting away from Damien. He scared me. I immediately thought, 'How is he going to get out of the cemetery? What was he doing there? Where did he come from? So strange, that I hadn't seen him earlier in the cemetery. What was he doing hanging around that old Cunningham mausoleum?'

Chapter 6

The next morning, I drove to my job as a middle school teacher but couldn't get Damien out of my mind. I wanted to share my experience with somebody but felt others would think I was making it all up. I then got an idea. What if Damian had something to do with the Cunningham mausoleum? He told me nobody was buried there, but when I looked in the window, I know I saw a casket. Somebody must have been buried there. If not, why was there a casket? Even more puzzling, why had the lid to the coffin been lifted off at some point? Who were the Cunninghams? What happened back around 1905 that led them to move after building that magnificent mausoleum? Tom Besore had told us that the Cunningham family relocated to California and that the mausoleum was empty.

On Monday afternoon, right after school, I drove over to the Oak Park Library on Lake Street. Walking in, I asked Information where I could find old newspapers. She directed me to their microfiche files, and I sat down to do some research.

I soon learned a bit more about the Cunninghams. They were a very wealthy merchant family who, in the 1880s, re-located to Chicago from Cleveland. In Cleveland, they had opened a successful department and now wanted to do the same in Chicago. Mr. Cunningham, having loved Chicago, moved to Oak Park to be close to the city and enjoy the beautiful tree-lined suburban life. He opened a major department store in downtown Chicago with the intent of competing with Marshall Field's and The Fair stores. Through good merchandising and a great product line, he quickly met with success and opened a second store in Oak Park, IL. In 1884, after courting a young Oak Park lady he quietly married her in a lovely June wedding.

They settled down and built a magnificent three-story house in a lovely section of Oak Park.. The mansion had a long curving drive and a two-story coach house nestled in the rear of the property. In 1885, they had their first and only child. It was listed in the birth notices of the Chicago Tribune that their son was born on September 8, 1885. His name... Damien.

Damien Cunningham to be exact.

Stunned. I sat there in the library staring off as my mind raced. It all seemed confusing.

I had to stop, close down the microfiche and go home. Now, mind you, I have never believed in ghosts, spirits or the supernatural. So, was it just a coincidence that I met somebody named Damien outside the Cunningham mausoleum? Why was he so 'different' looking?

The following day while teaching, I kept thinking about the strange circumstances of the empty mausoleum and the appearance of someone named Damien. I knew I had to learn more. I just had to know more. I resolved to go back to the Oak Park Library after school and continue my research.

Later, after school, I went back to the library to continue my research. Putting my pad of paper and pen down, I once again began a search through old newspapers from that early period of time. I learned that Mrs. Cunningham was very involved in Oak Park community organizations, including this library. I learned that the Cunninghams, along with young Damien, went on a European vacation in 1894 and spent a week in Switzerland. The article stated that Damien visited every natural history museum he could find. I was hoping I could find more information about him.

As I scrolled down in the microfiche, I gasped to read that tragedy struck the Cunninghams. They had a fire in their home in 1904. Not just a fire, but a horrible incident leading to the death of young Damien.

It took place on April 24, 1904. According to accounts from back then, I learned that young Damien had arrived home from school around 1:30 that afternoon. He was attending class at Oak Park High School, and there had been an early dismissal. The articles stated that normally when Damien arrived from school, there would be a nanny waiting for him, and she would stay to prepare dinner for the Cunningham family. That afternoon, however, the nanny had requested permission to take the day off for personal reasons.

Apparently, Damien had gone up to his 3rd floor bedroom which overlooked the tree-lined backyard. It was believed the fire was due to an electrical fault. Electrical wiring was still rather new back then, and though Thomas Edison came up with the idea of a circuit breaker in 1879, they were not found to be in common use in many homes. The fire at the Cunningham home was thought to have broken out in a wall sconce in the 3rd floor stairway. Damien, being alone in his bedroom on the 3rd floor, had no to way to escape. His bedroom windows faced toward the rear of the property, so even if he had called for help, it was unlikely his voice could be heard.

The obituary stated that there was a private memorial for Damien at the Cunningham residence. I can imagine the overwhelming grief felt by his parents as he was their own child. Since it was a fire, I felt sure it was probably a closed casket. Could that be the same opened coffin, I saw in the below ground crypt?

Chapter 7

My first thought after learning of a young Damien being lost in a house fire was to wonder if it is possible that there is a connection with the young man named Damien, I met at the cemetery. I regretted that there was no picture in the newspapers of the young Damien lost in the fire. I wondered where I might find a picture of him. I learned that he had attended classes at Oak Park High School. Perhaps, if I could find an early yearbook from there dating back to 1904, I could see the 'real Damien.'

On Wednesday after school, I drove over to the Oak Park River Forest High School. I knew the principal who had attended the same university I had, and we were good friends. I asked him if he might be able to find a yearbook from 1904, and he said he would do the best he could and get back to me. On Thursday afternoon, while my class was attending an assembly, my cellphone rang. It was the principal friend of mine, and he had good news. He had found the old yearbook and was holding it for me in his office.

It was with great anticipation that Thursday, after school, I drove over to look at the yearbook. My friend had to leave but had left the yearbook for me in the office. He said it was the only copy he could find, so I had to be extra careful handling it and to return it as soon as I was done.

I took the yearbook down to the high school library and, with my hands shaking, began turning the pages. At the end of the book was an index,and when I looked up the name Damien Cunningham, I found three page numbers listed. The first one was a page for a numismatic club, and there were four pictures of students sitting at desks looking at coins and stamps. There it was, a picture of approximately seven students gathered at a long table looking down at a series of coins laid out. In the back row all the way to the left was Damien. The picture showed a young man with sandy hair, glasses, not-smiling and looking down. I kept staring at his picture, but I couldn't say for sure if it was the same Damien from the cemetery.

Then, turning to the next picture listed in the index of the yearbook, I found another grouping of pictures with young boys staring at a wall of glass encased insects. At the top of the page in bold print, it read "BUG BOYS EXPANDING THEIR KNOWLEDGE." I am sure the yearbook editor must have put that in for jest. A small article at the bottom of the page informed the reader that the students in the pictures had, two years previous, discovered an insect never before seen or classified by anyone.

Taking my time to read the names of the boys in the pictures, I soon saw that Damien was again off to the left in one of the pictures, and only his profile was showing as he, like the other bug boys, was looking at a display of butterflies on a wall. It was this picture that did it for me. That profile. I kept looking at it, wondering just why it seemed familiar to me, and then I realized it was the same nose and set of the jaw. The picture in the yearbook showed a young man with a ski nose, kind of like Richard Nixon, and a weak jaw. Those features were the same as the young man in the Forest Home Cemetery.

Finally, my hands still shaking, I looked at the final picture of him in the yearbook. This one was a class picture of students, taken individually, and in the middle of the page I spotted him. Yes, no doubt this picture was of the same young man. He was wearing glasses, his sandy hair brushed straight back, and he had a discernable ski nose. No smile again, but it was obvious he was camera shy. Yes, no doubt of it. The photos I saw in the yearbook were of the same young man in the cemetery.

Now, it all began to make sense. The burnt-looking wrinkled skin, the smell of ashes, the stiff spiky black hair, the old faded clothes and top coat. Even his presence by the Cunningham mausoleum on a late Sunday afternoon, his bony crinkly hand, the coffin in the crypt with the top open.

Why was I singled out by him?

Chapter 8

I have never believed in spirits, ghosts or the supernatural. Yet, how could I explain this? I wished I could tell somebody about this, but who? The few friends I had would think it was too strange to be real and wouldn't believe me. The police? They would laugh me out of the station, and what could I expect them to do?

The one thing I began to think about was Damien perishing alone in his bedroom that fateful afternoon. It interested me to learn he was a 'coin collector,' because I am one too. I began collecting coins when I was around 11 years old and remain one to this day. Thinking back on his death in 1904, I began to think of all the coins that may have been popular to collectors back then. How many new coins had been minted that he never got to see, like the buffalo nickel, the mercury dime, the walking liberty half dollar?

I then had an idea. I would go back out to the cemetery with some old coins and try and use them as a connection between him and myself. Yes, I know it sounds strange to even think that, but one thing I know about us coin collectors is that we can be 'strange,' and we have this innate ability to appreciate coin designs and dates.

Hopefully, it wouldn't be painful to talk to Damien about coins, as it could cause him to think back to those youthful days when he was alive. Okay, now I am getting too weird here. Damien, if he is still living in the cemetery, is a spirit. How on earth could that be? Could he do me harm? Am I the only one to have seen and talked to him? Why did he talk to me? Is he visible to others who pass through the cemetery?

Friday afternoon, on my way home from teaching, I drove slowly past the Forest Home Cemetery. I could see the iron gate was closed, so that helped me to decide not to try and enter as it was closing. Tomorrow, being a quiet Saturday, I knew I would have to return. My intent was to engage him and try to learn more.

On getting home, I pulled out a metal box of old coins I kept in my closet. Sitting on the floor with a cup of coffee, I began to sort out my old coins and determine what may interest somebody who had unexpectedly left earthly life back in 1904. Grabbing an annual Red Book of Coins from 2010 and a selection of coins representing the Lincoln cent, Standing Liberty Quarter, a Mercury dime along with the Roosevelt dime, I then thought of the Peace Dollar from 1921 and how interesting that might be, for when he was alive the Morgan Dollar was in use. The Peace Dollar resulted from peace following WWI. He had died before that terrible war.

Chapter 9

The next morning, Saturday, I awoke to a rainy day. I made myself a cup of coffee and looked out the kitchen window. I watched the rain come down as the cool fall breeze was blowing the last of the brown autumn leaves. I thought of how much easier it would be to grab my copy of the newly delivered NY Times, take my coffee and sit down in an easy chair by the living room window. Should I drive over to the cemetery? Would he even be out on a day like this? I wondered where Damien went on days like this? Does he crawl through the window back into the dark, damp crypt? If so, what's down there other than the dusty old coffin? Thinking these thoughts depressed me.

How many autumns has he spent alone out in the cemetery? What does he do on cold, wintry days when the temperature drops to below zero and the wind picks up to blizzard force? A million questions began to flood through my mind.

When did he first learn he could leave his coffin? Has he ever talked to others? Am I the first one? Does he eat? Does he experience loneliness? Okay, I thought, just have my coffee, and if the rain lets up, I will drive back to the Forest Home Cemetery. In the meantime, just as I settled down to listen to the pitter patter against the window, I found myself thinking of all the history that had taken place from that Wednesday afternoon on April 27, 1904. I felt I could not completely rest without seeing him again.

The rain never did let up that day, and in fact, it came down even harder which caused me to decide to stay home that Saturday. I told myself that tomorrow, I would get to Forest Home, just as soon as the iron gate swung open. This time, I would try and take a picture of him.

Sunday morning, I woke up, made breakfast, grabbed the old coins and Red Book along with my camera/phone and headed out the door. A half hour later, pulling in through the iron gate around noon, I drove up the old narrow concrete drive to the Cunningham Mausoleum.

Looking around, I didn't see a single person. The grass was still wet from yesterday, the air was clear and fresh, and silence was complete. I felt a trepidation walking through the leaf-strewn wet grass, and as I approached, I looked around to see if I could see him. Nothing! I was alone. Cemeteries can be such lonely places. You can't help but look out at a multitude of graves and think each one represents a now deceased soul. Each of them once had their own hopes, dreams, desires, loves, wishes. Each one holds the bones of a person who had seen the same sun as I, felt the same chill of winter as I, gone to sleep with the anticipation of waking up to a new day, felt the grief of losing a family member or friend.

Now, their bones lay there as testimony that they had once been born, lived and died.

Standing there at the Cunningham grave site, I thought of the overwhelming sadness Damien's mother and father must have experienced right here, where I was now standing, but 100 years earlier.

Walking around the mausoleum, I wanted to get down on the ground and look into the window, down into the crypt to see if maybe, perhaps… could he be down there???

Immediately, I decided to not do so as the grass was wet, and along the concrete wall of the crypt it was muddy. I felt almost silly, standing there and tempted to call out the name 'Damien.' I knew nobody would hear me because, from what I could see, I was the only living soul around. On the top platform of the crypt were two granite benches. So, climbing up the three steps leading to it, I walked over, took out my handkerchief and wiped it down and sat on the cool damp stone. I looked at my watch and saw it was only 12:30 pm. I decided to give myself until 2:00 to see if he showed up. Pulling out my phone, I sat there on that granite bench and looked out over the myriad shapes of grave stones.

By 1:30, I had only seen one person off in the distance walking through the cemetery. They were so far away, I couldn't make out if it was a man or woman. Getting chilled on that granite bench and the cool autumn air, I wished I had brought a cup of coffee. At 2:00, I stood up, stretched and decided to walk around the cemetery and come back in a while to see if he was here.

Chapter 10

So, walking back down the three steps, I headed off to series of graves I had seen when I had pulled in. The graves had intrigued me, for it was obviously a German family grave site. All the names were German, and the mother and father's head stones read, 'Mutter' and 'Vater.' They had six children and, reading the headstones, I could see that one had died on December 9, 1923. Sadly, that stone read, "Our Boy." It was that of an eight-year-old boy who had died and was buried with his extended family members. I often get too sentimental, but looking at the young boy's headstone, I tried to imagine his family standing there, shedding tears and heading home afterwards, 16 days before Christmas, to grieve his passing.

I then saw a car pull in and slowly travel down the single lane road. Glancing at the car, I could see an elderly couple inside, looking very stone-faced. I wondered who they were here to see. This was an old cemetery where many of the older graves were German, from the turn of the 19th century. Many of them had Mason signs on them. The car continued down the old concrete road and I did not see it again.

Growing up, my family would visit the cemetery, maybe once a month, to put fresh flowers on our loved ones' graves. My mother taught us to always bow our heads and say a prayer, and we were not allowed to run around or show any irreverence. My grandfather had come to America from Ireland and had a 12 foot tall concrete Celtic cross constructed in the cemetery, where he was interred. Of his 8 children, 6 of them and their spouses are buried there with him and my grandmother. Several times a year, as a child, we would visit, place flowers and pray for them.

After that car passed, I looked around, and not a soul was in sight. How times have changed. Walking past the old headstones, I did not see any fresh flowers. These souls in the damp ground and in their stone mausoleums were forgotten.

Around 3:30, I walked back to the Cunningham Mausoleum. I knew the cemetery would be closing at 4:30, and I held my breath, hoping I might see Damien. Approaching the huge stone monument, I did not see anybody. Walking around it, I had an idea. I walked over to the bar-less window and got down close to the ground to see if I could see any footprints. I thought I was being very clever but to no avail. There wasn't a single footprint near the windows, and other than weeds, leaves and a few broken twigs, I could find no evidence that anybody else had been there.

Disappointed, yet for some strange reason, feeling relieved, I decided to just leave, but then I remembered the coins in my pocket. Should I leave any of them here? If so, where? I actually considered taking the little baggy I had the coins in and throwing it through the open window down into the crypt. I figured that if I threw hard enough I could get them to land near the empty coffin. Then I could come by next week, lay prone on the ground, and using my camera flashlight, I could see if the coins were still there.

Pausing to ponder that idea, it dawned on me that I may just be throwing the coins away, for they might stay there on that concrete floor of the crypt forever. Furthermore, I reasoned, what if the coins were gone, and my purpose of bringing the coins was to try and make a connection? I thought to myself, "Okay, leave the book and some of the old coins on the inside window ledge of the crypt."That way, I presumed, next week, I could open the unlocked window, reach in, and see if the coins were on the ledge or not. The 2010 Red Book is a guide to coins from the earliest American coins to present day and I was hoping Damien would like looking through it.

Opening the baggy, I pulled out five old coins dating from 1905 and, reaching my hand through the propped open window, I gently laid them and the red book on the inside ledge of the crypt. Then, slowly letting the window close, I got up, brushed off the wet leaves and, giving one last look around, walked back toward my car.

Getting in my car, I turned it around and drove slowly toward the old iron gate.

Chapter 11

Driving home a bit disappointed, I began to seriously question my sighting of Damien. I told myself to put him out of my mind, concentrate on teaching and try and forget about him.

The following weekend was an intercity chess match, and as I was my school's chess club advisor, I spent the week prepping my students. The next weekend came; I busied myself at the tournament held at Navy Pier along Chicago's lakefront. Following that were the upcoming Parent-Teacher Conferences, and life went on with me giving little thought to Damien.

It was now mid-November, and Thanksgiving was approaching. One thought kept coming up in my mind, and that was the coins I had left in the crypt and of Damien. I resolved to go back there one more time and see for myself if he was there or not.

The Wednesday before Thanksgiving was an early dismissal at my school. I left for my extended weekend around 1:30 in the afternoon and headed back to the Forest Home Cemetery.

It had begun snowing earlier that morning and continued as I pulled away from school. By the time I reached the cemetery there had to have been at least three inches of snow. Pulling in through the gate, I could see the old concrete drive had not been plowed, and so I had to drive slowly toward the Cunningham Mausoleum. Getting out of my car, the air seemed muffled as it does after a blanket of snow. Not having boots, I picked my way through the snow and up ahead could see the imposing mausoleum. In doing so, I passed by the old German grave site with the headstone of the 8-year-old boy who had died in 1927. I paused, bowed my head, and said a prayer for him. I know on days like this, a snowfall, time off of school for Thanksgiving would have been a time for him to celebrate and, like any 8-year-old boy, go out to play. Sad…

My feet were getting cold and wet. The air was still and so quiet I could almost hear the snow falling. If I really listened, I could just barely hear the sound of a train in the far distance. Walking to the window where I had placed the coins, I saw no footprints in the snow. I bent down, laid flat on the cold snow, and with my left hand pushed the window open. Then, with my right hand, I reached in to feel along the inside window ledge for the coins and book. They were gone. In my excitement, I almost let the open window close on my hand. I again reached in and began feeling around on the cold stone ledge, but there was nothing.

Did Damien take them? I know they couldn't have fallen off the ledge, as it was at least six inches wide. Then I thought I could hear a soft humming sound. Getting my head down closer toward the window opening, I listened again. For sure, there was a soft humming sound coming from the crypt. It was a raspy-sounding humming. I knew it had to be Damien.

Smiling to hear him humming, I quietly closed the window, stood up, brushed the snow off of myself and decided to leave. Who was I to disturb the deceased? I could not change what happened to Damien any more than I could change the fate of that 8-year-old German boy who had died in 1923. Damien still haunts his crypt.

Once in a while, I think back to Damien but have resolved to never try and make a connection to those on the 'other side.' As they say,

RIP. I have peace of mind in having heard Damien humming that cold day in November, for I know he is resting in peace.

Author Page

James C Boland, born in Odgen, Utah has spent most of his life in the midwest. He served 2 tours of duty as a Marine in Vietnam and upon discharge went back to college, where he earned a BA and MBA. He went on to have a successful career as an entrepreneur but decided to make a career change in 1996. Going back to college he got a Masters in Education and became a teacher in Chicago. He has taught as an adjunct college instructor, along with a teacher in high school, junior high and elementary. Upon retiring in 2008, Mr. Boland, went on to substitute teach in over 80 schools. His teaching experiences taught him that children love stories. This is Mr. Boland's first scary book.

DAMIEN is fiction but it is based on a real life incident that occurred at the Forest Home Cemetery.

Richard Flatley, like Mr. Boland is a Marine veteran who also served in Vietnam. He and Mr. Boland became friends many years after their shared experience of serving as Marines. Richard Flatley, as an illustrator, loves to draw and has done illustrations in books, magazines and promotional material. The two of them have a shared love for story telling. Mr. Boland and Mr. Flatley collaborated on their first published book in August 2019

Mr. Boland and Mr. Flatley have both pledged that a portion of the profits from this book will be donated to the Friends of the Fisher House in Illinois.

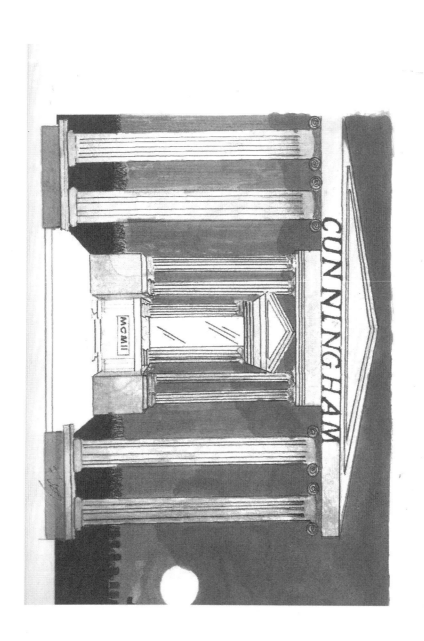

Made in the USA
Columbia, SC
29 March 2021

35205219R10022